DISNEY · PIXAR

Cars

MATER'S BIRTHDAY SURPRISE

P9-DCC-715

By Melissa Lagonegro

Illustrated by the Disney Storybook Artists

Random House 🏠 New York

It is Mater's birthday.
His friends
are planning
a surprise party.

It is a secret!

Lightning is in charge.

Everyone gets a job.

Luigi blows up balloons.

He uses his tire pump.

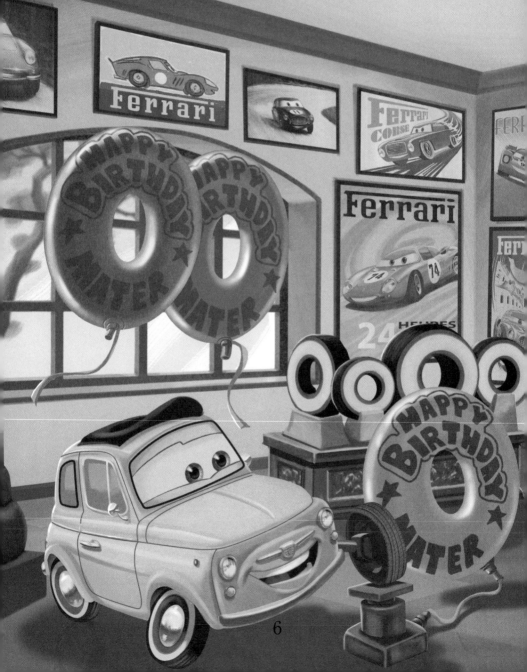

Guido makes

a pretend tire cake.

Fillmore makes a batch
of his tasty fuel.
Mater loves it.

Jeff Gorvette races
to the party.
He does not want
to be late.

Lightning sets up
the party games.
Mater loves games.

He likes

Pin the Bumper

on the Car.

Sally wraps presents.
Mater wants
a new tow hook
and a rusty hubcap.

Honk
for
Service

Flo picks out
streamers and bows.
Red uses his ladder
to hang them.

Ramone paints
a birthday sign.

Mater's friends arrive!
Sarge leads them
to the party.

They are very quiet.
They don't want Mater
to hear them.

HERE
IT IS

Finn and Holley come for the party!

They are on

a top-secret mission.

They bring Mater

a new disguise.

The party begins!

Presents are piled up.

Streamers hang down.

Mater is coming!
The cars hide!
Lightning looks
for Mater.

Surprise!

It is not Mater!

It is Lizzie.

She has the party hats.

Where is Mater?

Lightning goes
to find him.
He looks
around town.

Sheriff looks,
too.
He searches
the back roads.

Lightning and Sheriff

come back

to the party.

They could not
find Mater.
Where is he?

Surprise!
Mater switches off
his new
present disguise.

His friends are

surprised instead.

Mater had fun
tricking his friends.

But he has
even more fun
at his party.
He plays games.

Happy birthday,
Mater!

Dear Parent:

Congratulations! Your child is taking the first steps on an exciting journey. The destination? Independent reading!

STEP INTO READING® will help your child get there. The program offers five steps to reading success. Each step includes fun stories and colorful art. There are also Step into Reading Sticker Books, Step into Reading Math Readers, Step into Reading Phonics Readers, Step into Reading Write-In Readers, and Step into Reading Phonics Boxed Sets—a complete literacy program with something to interest every child.

Learning to Read, Step by Step!

Ready to Read   Preschool–Kindergarten
• big type and easy words • rhyme and rhythm • picture clues
For children who know the alphabet and are eager to begin reading.

Reading with Help   Preschool–Grade 1
• basic vocabulary • short sentences • simple stories
For children who recognize familiar words and sound out new words with help.

Reading on Your Own   Grades 1–3
• engaging characters • easy-to-follow plots • popular topics
For children who are ready to read on their own.

Reading Paragraphs   Grades 2–3
• challenging vocabulary • short paragraphs • exciting stories
For newly independent readers who read simple sentences with confidence.

Ready for Chapters   Grades 2–4
• chapters • longer paragraphs • full-color art
For children who want to take the plunge into chapter books but still like colorful pictures.

STEP INTO READING® is designed to give every child a successful reading experience. The grade levels are only guides. Children can progress through the steps at their own speed, developing confidence in their reading, no matter what their grade.

Remember, a lifetime love of reading starts with a single step!

For Lilly and Lucy —M.L.

Step into Reading, Random House, and the Random House colophon are registered trademarks of Random House, Inc.

Visit us on the Web!
StepIntoReading.com
randomhouse.com/kids

Educators and librarians, for a variety of teaching tools, visit us at
randomhouse.com/teachers

ISBN: 978-0-7364-2858-3 (trade) — ISBN: 978-0-7364-8098-7 (lib. bdg.)

Printed in the United States of America 10 9 8 7 6 5 4 3 2

Random House Children's Books supports the First Amendment and celebrates the right to read.